Paper Girls

1

BRIAN K. VAUGHAN writer
CLIFF CHIANG artist
MATT WILSON colors
JARED K. FLETCHER letters

image

Jared K. Fletcher - Logo + Book Design

PAPER GIRLS, VOL. 1. Second printing. December 2016. Published by Image Comics, Inc. Office of publication: 2001 Center Street, Sixth Floor, Berkeley, CA 94704.

ISBN: 978-1-63215-674-7

Is this...?
Yes,
Erin.

Welcome to Heaven.
You're her.
You're *Christa McAuliffe.*
That's right. Everyone from the *Challenger* is here. And so is your Gram. But not your fish, okay?
My fish. I drowned, didn't I?
No, it was the Russians. They got almost everybody.
Then... where's my sister?
Oh, Missy is in Hell.

What?!
But you still have one chance to save her.
UH-HUH.
ALL YOU HAVE TO DO IS ANSWER MY QUESTION.
aoduf hoaw ehfie qwugf
I don't understand!
YOU HAVE ONE MINUTE.
1) WHICH TRIBE NAMED OUR "CROOKED RIVER" THE CUYAHOGA?
A) THE MOHAWKS
B) THE IROQUOIS
C) THE APACHE
D) THE BLACKFEET
Fuck you.

WHAT DID YOU SAY?
I've had this dream before.
It...it isn't even real, so it doesn't count if I swear in here.
INCORRECT.
Please.
WE WARNED YOU...NEVER EAT FROM THE TREE OF KNOWLEDGE.
NASA
CHRISTA

MONSTER SQUAD
Missy?
Are you dead?

The Cleveland Preserver
· 1988 ·
NOVEMBER
1
Tuesday
Hell morning!!!
uch for the rest of them?"

Preserver
VOL. CXXXIX... No. 49,623
NO PROGRESS IN IRA
IRAQ PEACE TALKS
Tuesday
ber 1, 1988
40 CE
Nov
4:40

RIP

Welcome to
STONY STREAM
OHIO
Yo!
RIP
RIP
Can I get one of those?
You skipped my house.

Teenagers.
Say what?
Um, what's your family's address?
Um, none of your business.
You're not a Stony Middle chick, are you?
No, I... I go to St. Nick's.
Yum, Catholic schoolgirl.
She's, like, eight, man.
Grass on the field...
I'm twelve.
And I have to get back to work.
Not until you give me a goddamn paper.
Lucas Kurzenberger!

Cool costume, faggot.

Excuse me?
You heard me, AIDS patient.
Get lost.
Or what?
Or I tell your gym coach of a dad that you were out past curfew, harassing little girls.
And I kick the shit out of you for being a *rat*.
Whatever.
Good luck getting home alive, bitch.
Can I have your grape Nerds?
Under no circumstances.

You okay?
You shouldn't call anyone the other F-word.
And anybody can get AIDS, not just gays.
...you're welcome?
Don't mind Mac.
Yeah, she just knows how to talk to their kind.
You know, ***Herbs.***
Wait, you're Mac?
As in, MacKenzie?
So what?
You were the first.
The first paperboy around here who wasn't a... you know.

Hey, I was the first altar girl long before Mac took over her brother's route.
Yeah, Tiffany's like the Amelia Earhart of crap that doesn't matter.
You guys are both in private, too?
Uh-huh.
I'm at St. Pete's, but KJ goes to to Buttonwood Academy with the rest of the heathens.
That is so anti-Semitic.
You rich girls want to compare report cards all night or can we get back to business?
So you three deliver together?
Just for All Saint's, 'cause there are so many crazies still out.
We met last Halloween, decided to team up. You can totally join us, too, if you want?
No, it'll take too long for all four of us to do the entire development together. We'll split up into two groups.
New kid can ride with me.

Um, it's Erin.
My name is--
Tiff, can we borrow one of your walkie-talkies?
This isn't a "walkie-talkie," it's a Realistic TRC-218 CB with channel 14 crystals.
Each one cost me $49.99, not counting tax or batteries, so if you lose it, you're hauling your butt to Radio Shack for a--
KRAKOOM
Perfect.
Forecast didn't say anything about rain today.
Like our paper ever gets the weather right.
Let's just get this over with. We'll meet back here at dawn.
Keep up, new kid.

You want to bum a Camel, just ask.
A cigarette? No way.
I mean, no thanks. My grandmother died of lung cancer.
Anyway... you have every house on Poplar?
All of 'em except 1833.
That bald creep stiffed me last time I came to collect, said he'd make it up to me next month. As if.
But, he's still in your subscription book, right?
Aren't we supposed to keep delivering until they cancel?
Our routes, our rules. I'm sick of shaking down deadbeats. Either pay us on time, or get your stupid sports page somewhere else.
Cool.

You know what would be cool? Still being *asleep* right now.
Well, I'm glad you're out here, Mac.
You, like, opened a door for lots of us.
Like it matters.
We're the last of a dying breed anyway.
What do you mean?
My dad says there's no future in newspapers.
We pretty much used up all the trees on the planet, so in a few years, everyone's just gonna get their news off the TV.
What, like *The Today Show*?
My mom likes Jane Pauley, but she thinks Bryant Gumbel is a--
COYLE!
Shit.

What the hell are you up to?
My job?
STONY STREAM
POLICE
Bull.
I got multiple reports of someone ***smashing windows*** in this development.
So what?
So, you getting into the family business?
I don't know what you're talking about, man.
You address me as ***Officer***, young lady.
And put out that cigarette before I write you up.
There's no law against me having smokes.
But there is one against underage brats like you ***buying*** them.
Good thing I got these trick-or-treating.
Ah, I've been with MacKenzie all night, Officer. She...she hasn't done anything wrong.

Keep it up, Coyle.
Sooner or later...
Sooner or later what?!
The police know you by name?
I guess.
Um... so what do cigarettes taste like, anyway?
kzzt enzie, help us! dzzk
KJ?
fzzt orner of Locust and Ash, and we're...STOP! Don't touch her! I'll gzzt
I know a shortcut through Spruce!
Come on!

Real brave, tough guys!
You all right?
What happened?
We got ***jumped*** by three guys in bad ghost costumes.
They grabbed Tiffany's other walkie.
I had to use almost all my Christmas tips to finally afford a second one.
Months of riding in the freezing cold down the drain.
Was it the same jerks who stopped me?
No, these guys were speaking Spanish or something.
KJ, I've taken three years of Spanish.
Whatever they were speaking, it ***wasn't*** that.

Who cares *where* these losers came from?
They're not getting away with this.
Mrs. Drobneck over on Acorn is usually up by now. We can ask her to call the police for us.
The same cops who think I'm a criminal?
Yeah, Stony PD is the worst.
I tried to report this weird lady following me in her station wagon one time, and the 911 operator just told me to call back when I had an "actual emergency."
So what do we do?
What do you think?
Hey, whichever dumb fucks just robbed our friend, if you can hear this, get ready...
...'cause we're coming to get our shit back.

You sure they went this way?
Pretty sure.
But it happened so fast. By the time Tiffany hit the pavement, they were almost to the woods.
Maybe they're hiding out in one of these unfinished houses.
My sister and I have snuck into some before.
There are always beer cans and stuff left over from people partying.
Vytek
Check it out.
Score.

We're not really going to *fight* these guys, are we?
If Tiff's stuff is broken, we're gonna *murder* them.
Holy...
What is that *stench?*
Smells like month-old barf in here.
Does anyone else hear that... hum?
Like how you can tell there's a TV on in your house, even if the volume's off?
Sounds like it's coming from downstairs.
Terrific.
Nothing spooky about basements.

Hello?
Dickweeds...?
Whoa.
The heck is that?

Help me get this sheet off.
Ew.
It feels kinda like... skin?
Yep, goodbye.
Tiffany, wait!
Nuh-uh. Flesh sheet?
That's some Texas Chainsaw bullshit.
It's not really skin... but it's not a sheet either.
It's connected to this thing.
Like a parachute.
Jesus.

It's like some kind of... modern art.
Yeah, it's *terrible.*
Where the hell did it even come from?
Outer space.

Shut up.
I'm not kidding.
This thing looks a lot like an old *Apollo capsule.*
I thought NASA was just using shuttles these days.
They are.
But maybe this thing came from Russia or something.
Or something?
Erin... what if it's *alien?*
Oh, come on. You dummies seriously don't realize what this is?
Am I the only one who actually *reads* the thing we deliver?

What are you talking about?
This is the fiftieth anniversary of War of the Worlds.
That stupid new TV show?
It was on the radio long before that.
This actor named, like, Orville Wright tried to trick everyone into believing there was a real alien invasion going on, and the whole country freaked out.
This is obviously just a rip-off of that hoax.
The guys who took Tiff's walkie wanted us to come here and find this stupid prop they built in shop class.
klang klang
Why?
Because we work for the newspaper.
These dorks figured we'd tell the Preserver that we found E.T.'s ship and help get them on TV's Bloopers & Practical Whatever.
But, how'd they even get it down here?
There's no way this thing could fit through that--
VMMMMMM

VMMMMMMMMMMMMMMMMMM
You hear that, right?
It's definitely getting--
Everybody okay?
No. And what happened to my--
VMMMMMMMMMMM
RUN.

KRSSHH
GO GO GO!
Is it gonna explode?
You want to wait around to find out?!
Still think this was a *prank?*
What do *you* think it was?
Some kind of... Martian nuke!
Why would Mars want to blow up a basement in *Cleveland?*
Whatever it is, it must have knocked out everybody's power. The streetlamps shouldn't have shut off this early.
Oh.
Oh my God.

I've never seen that many stars in my life.
I guess everything looks brighter up there when it's pitch black down here.
No way. The constellations have *never* looked like that, not even when I've been camping.
Guys.
It's them.
Vytek
HEY!

They're booking!
Kaje, wait!
Why are you doing this?!
Just give us back our--

Uhf
AHH!
Son of a bitch.
SON OF A BITCH!
Hit a girl?!
Gonna rip your eyes out of your...

ghh
Put.
Put...
her...

THUNK
VURVURVURVURRR

hwuhhh
Mac...?
She's in shock. But you...you saved her life.
whatishappening whatishappening whatishappening whatishappening whatishappening
VUR VUR VUR
Nah, whatever that noise is scared it off.
And look.
That thing dropped something.
What is it?
Seems like a... compact?
Got some kinda weird symbol on the back.
It's not a symbol.

It's an apple.

GEORGE
BUSH '88
WARNING
NEIGHBORHOOD WATCH
PROGRAM IN FORCE
WE IMMEDIATELY REPORT
ALL SUSPICIOUS ACTIVITIES

VUR VUR
VUR
VUR VUR

VUR VUR VUR VURRRRRRRRR

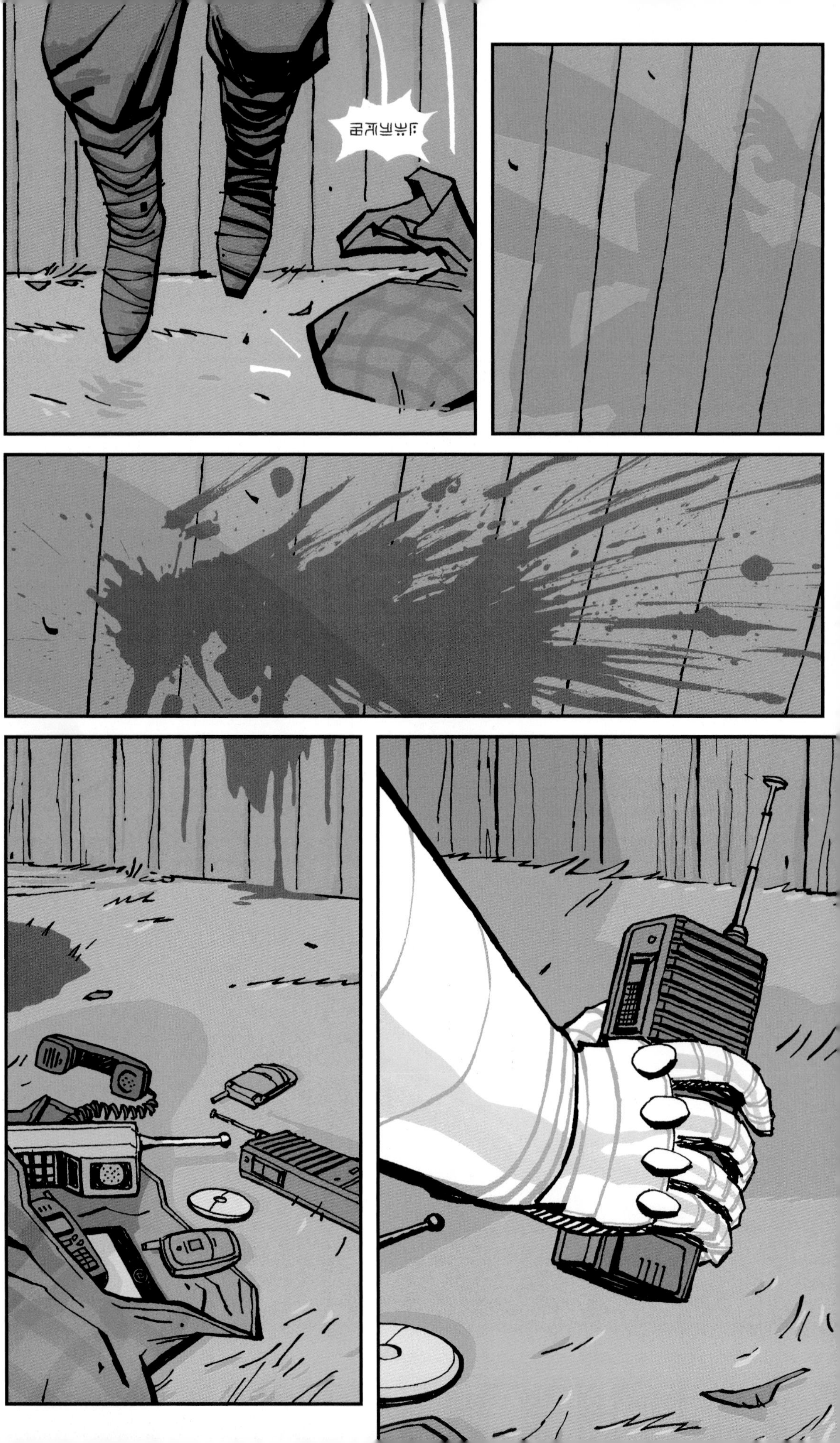

Mom!
Dad?
Anyone...?
Maybe your parents already left for work, Erin.
But, what about my sister? Missy always goes to school with *me.*
After all the insane crap going on? Your family probably got the hell out of Stony Stream.
Oh my god!

You guys give out *full-size* Hershey bars?
Oh, yeah, I think my mom is trying to make the neighbors like us.
Our neighbors don't like us.
HERSHEY'S MILK CHOCOLATE
Jesus, how can you two think about candy when the town's being overrun by *monsters?*
There's no such thing as monsters, Mac.
Are you joking? Did you even *see* what attacked us?
I did, and he looked like a person born with a...a *disease,* you know? Like Rocky Dennis?
Rocky Who?
From that movie? *Mask?* With Eric Stoltz?
Do I have a concussion? Because I am understanding zero percent of her words right now.
Huhh huhh huhh!
Ahh... what the heck is that?

It almost sounds like... laughing?
So now those evil freaks are **taunting** us?
What do I say back?
Nothing, Tiffany.
This is the part where we call the police.
Way ahead of you.
But there's no dial tone, just that emergency broadcast sound.
I'm telling you, everybody must have gotten the order to **evacuate.**
And they left **without** us?
Maybe our folks figured one of the dispatch trucks already picked us up.
Like in the blizzard last year?
Either way, we should get to my house.
My dad has a **gun.**

A gun? Like, a *real* one?
What other choice do we have, Tiff? Those things obviously aren't scared of KJ's shillelagh.
My what?
Hold on, what was the very first thing the *Preserver* told us when they gave us our bags?
We aren't the news, we don't even *report* the news, we just get the news where it needs to be.
If we see bad stuff happen, we're supposed to stay back and let the adults handle it.
The adults already blew this popsicle stand, new kid.
So you can hide out here and wait for those Frankensteins to break in and rape your face, but *I'm* gonna find a way to defend myself.
Who's with me?

You don't believe those were monsters... do you, KJ?
I don't know, but they definitely weren't good guys.
Maybe they're, like, some kind of nuclear mutants the Russians sent here from Chernobyl.
What if they're from a lot farther away than that?

Because of that fruity thing they dropped?
It has a logo a lot like the one on the **computer** my school got last year.
I've been thinking, what if this is some kind of...**micro version** of it?
How would you fit an entire computer inside something the size of a Klondike bar?
Well, thirty years ago, computers used to fill up entire rooms.
Maybe they'll get even smaller in the **future.**
Back up, you think we're being invaded by, what...**time travelers?**
And that's less dumb than monsters **how,** Erin?
It's at least **sort of** scientifically possible. I mean, what if the people who jumped us used that **capsule thing** we found to slingshot around the sun?
You know, like in *Star Trek IV?*
Yeah, sorry, I'm not really into science fiction flicks. Unless you count *Peggy Sue Got Married?*
That's actually more of a **fantasy** time travel story than--
Hey, Siskel and Ebert, would you please zip it?
We're supposed to be keeping our eyes peeled for--
GUYS!

errrrrrrrrrrrt
STOP
Is...is that...?
I think it's Wallace Bund.

Who?
Eighth grader.
He brought a **mask** exactly like that to school yesterday.
Why's he just standing there like a creep?
He's kind of a creep.
What's up, Wally?
Don't get close to him, Tiff!
What if it's another one of those... whatever!
It's definitely him.
I can smell his gross Drakkar Noir from here.
This is kind of a terrible idea!
Please, let's keep moving!

We just want to know what the heck is going on.
Where did everybody go?
Don't make me rip that stupid thing off your--
VUR VUR
VURVURVURRRRRRRRRRR
Oh, no.
That's the sound... the sound that scared off that other freak-show.
VUR VUR VUR
Where the hell is it coming from?!
All around us!
No.
Not around us.

What.
What the ***fuck?***
...monsters...
We can't be out here.
No duh.
Tiffany, let's go!
But we can't just leave...
...Wallace?
Where--
He obviously booked, like ***we*** should!
Come on, my house isn't far!
We'll be ***safe*** there.

...I've never... pedaled so fast... in my *life...*
If I hadn't already puked up breakfast today, I'd be doing it now.
You think any of those flying things *saw* us?
If they did, they didn't come after us.
Yet.
But like we say in the Scouts, "Be prepared."
Wait, you used to be a *Girl Scout?*
I still am.
Why, you want to be a bitch about it?
Watch your language, young lady.

That mouth of yours is probably why you're still here.
Alice?
You know this lady?
She'd better.
I'm MacKenzie's ***mom.***

Actually, Alice is my ***stepmother.***
She met my dad in A.A.
Which part of ***anonymous*** don't you understand?
I don't know, which part of ***not drinking*** don't you understand?
Hn.
What difference does it make now? Don't know if you and your friends have noticed, but the G.D. ***world*** is ending.
Um, your...your stepdaughter said we could hide from those creatures in here, ma'am.
Kid, I have no idea who you are, but don't ever call me the M-word.
Makes me feel a thousand years old.
And those things aren't "creatures," they're ***demons.***
Demons from You-Know-Where.
Alice, where's my dad?

He's gone.
Forever.
What are you--
I was dozing next to him in bed when this, this awful **sound** woke us both up, and then...
...then I watched my husband just, just **vanish.** Disappeared into thin air.
Wallace.
Your father was a good man, which is why he got sucked up to Heaven.
See, 'cause of Dukakis and... and all those people, we're finally living through that Bible thing that predicted this was gonna happen.
What the hell are you **talking** about? **What** Bible thing?
I forget exactly what it's called.
Maybe if I'd ever opened the damn book...
...I wouldn't be stranded here with the rest of you sinners.

Alice, please.
Please put that down.
There's only one thing the Lord wants us to do here, you understand that, right?
Look, we don't know exactly what's happening out there, but it doesn't have anything to do with God.
Trust me, I...I've gone to Catholic school my whole life.
Yeah, I thought I knew everything when I was your age, too.
I hated being twelve. Back in '65, I just wanted to grow up fast so everything would finally be good, you know?
But truth is, life was actually way better back then. Turns out, the older you get...the more everything just turns to *shit*.
You girls are lucky you'll never have to find that out.
DON'T!

UHN!
Mac, be careful!
You can't do this!
I =hnn= have to, sweetheart.
But I love you.
Mom, I lo--
BANG

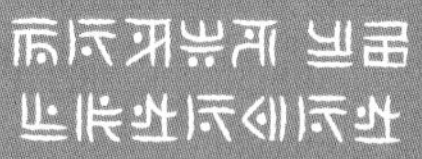

Whoa.
SPIDERS FOOTBALL
I am tripping my face off.
TERRY!

STONY STREAM HIGH SCHOOL
Terry, what the hell is this?!
Gabs?
You... you can see it, too?
There are *dragons* coming out of the sky!
Jesus H.
What happened to everybody else?
I was smoking under the stands with Becky and Tonia, and then it was like they just...*vanished.*
They musta got sucked through the gateway.
The *what?!*
Don't worry, Gabrielle. I'll keep you safe.

What is *wrong* with you?
I don't even *like* you like that, you psycho!
Besides, we have to concentrate on--
Is it because you're still into *Chris?*
'Cause Chris is probably *dead,* like everybody else in the whole damn Stream.
Get away from me.
Whatever this is, it's all happening for a *reason.*
I have wanted you since freshman year, and now we can finally--
Huhh huhh huhh!

Scruddy teenagers.

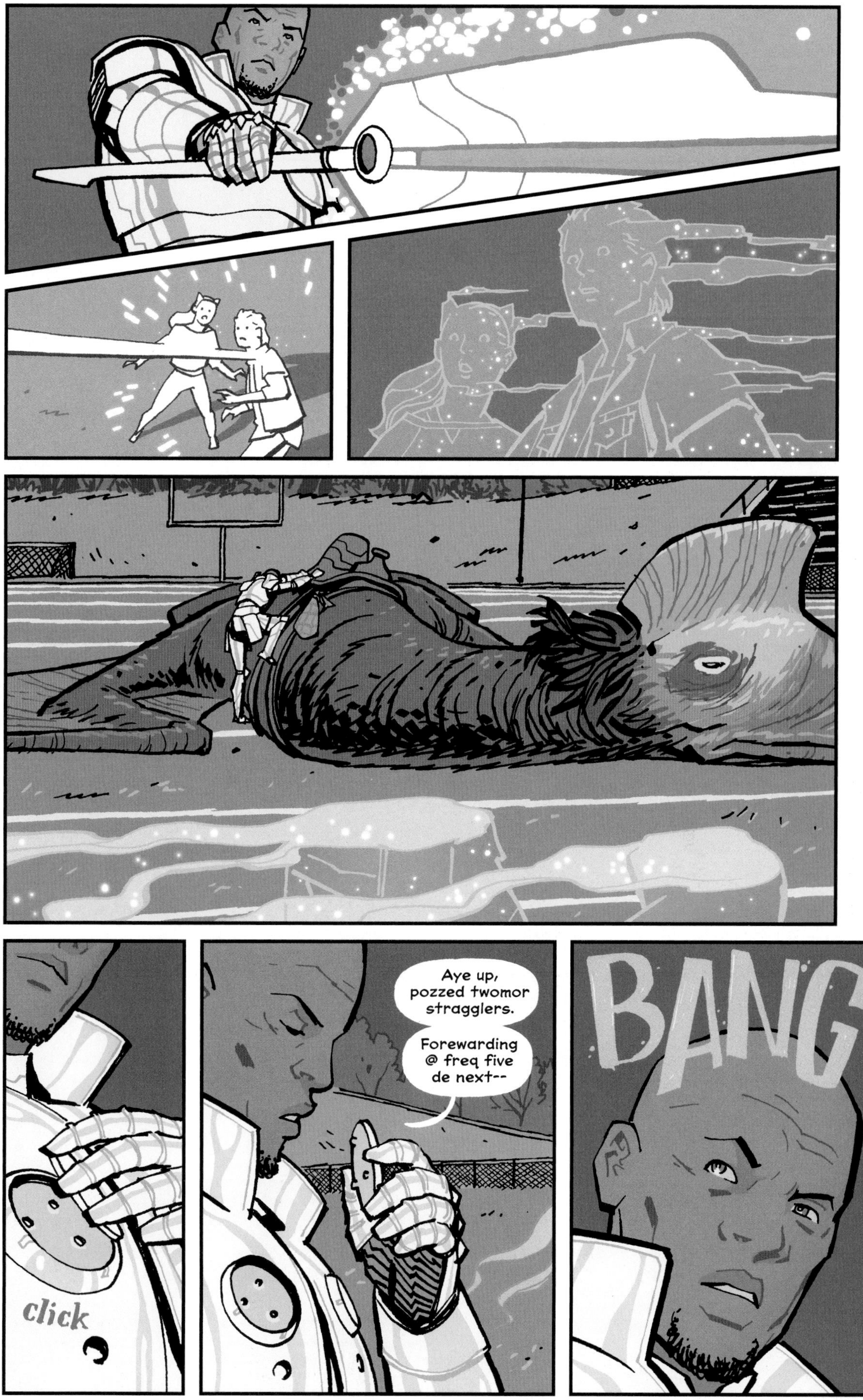
click
Aye up, pozzed twomor stragglers.
Forewarding @ freq five de next--
BANG

It...it just went off.
I wanted to get it away from you and it--
Is everyone all right?!
We're fine, ma'am.
Mac's shot must have gone right past us.
It's a miracle.

Erin?
thunk
Oh.
Holy crap!
What do we do?!
I know some first aid.
I can keep pressure on her stomach while my stepmom drives us to the hospital.
Um, about her...

What?
Alice *left?!*
Or maybe she got disappeared like everybody else.
Whatever, we have to get Erin to a hospital *now.*
On what, our handle-bars?
She's got a point, Tiff. We can't exactly call an ambulance while the phones are dead.
Then *I'll* drive us.
You're *twelve.*
So are you, dork!
And my dad's let me steer around his parking lot before, KJ. I'm pretty sure I remember how.
Good enough.
Just don't forget the *gun.*

Nuh-uh!
We are *not* bringing that thing with us!
What are you, MacGyver? It's the whole reason we came here!
And look how that turned out!
This wasn't my fault, Tiffany!
Besides, there are still deformed freaks and... and *giant killer birds* and who knows what other horrible--
Guys?
I'm gonna vote...no more bullets... please...
Yeah. Yeah, right.
You just hang in there, okay, new kid?
You're in awesome hands.

OHIO
212 BKY
Can't this half a station wagon go any faster?
You want me to honk the horn, too?
If I rev this ancient engine, I'm afraid one of those dino-things will swoop down and pick us up by the luggage rack.
Relax, it's like before.
If they even notice us up there, they don't seem to care.
But they will...because entropy.
That's one of our vocab words, right?
For the quiz tomorrow?

She's getting worse. How close are we?
Like, in miles?
I have no idea. I'm just going the way my mom goes to work.
Your mother's a nurse?
No, she's a *doctor*, and if she hasn't been alien-abducted like everybody else, she's going to save Erin's--
Huhh huhh huhh!
Great, and now the giggling a-holes who stole our other walkie are back.
Ye's ben twentied, jungs. KZZT Renders now or B same-fated as thy frend.
Say *what?*
I don't know, but that's definitely not the same language the creeps who jumped us were speaking.
Maybe these are *new* creeps?
Then what happened to the old ones?
The Cleveland Preserver
The Cleveland Preserver

The Cleveland Preserver

Snap out of it, Erin.
Remember when you spaced in Social Studies last week?
CCCP
What... what does this one mean?
Are we all dead?
No, it's like Dad said.
Not everyone who gets shot dies.

Why is God letting this happen to me?
We know the answer to that.
We've known since you realized it about Santa.
I miss fifth grade.
That's because you had *friends* back then.
I still do.
Your little sister doesn't count.
...what about Wendy?
Your *pen pal?*
That's just sad, Erin.
Now come on, you have an important job to do.
Remember your papers.

rgnn
You gotta stay awake.
Please.
--for thine mortal-plus syns, U will paye de charge ultimo...
...& all of thine fellow ratpacks shall B same-subjected.
What does all that bad Shakespeare mean?
I don't know, but would you please turn it down before I accidentally wrap us around a--
BRAKES!
RAILROAD CROSSING
HOP

SCREEEEEEEEEEEEEE
Huhh huhh huhh.
What is *this* guy?!
Stay with Erin.
I'll...I'll try talking to him.
No-know how U *lurked* solong, but endcredits for de lot, masters.
Ur transgresses willn't B--
Please, this girl we work with was *shot* and you please have to help us, please!
Hold.
R ye... *locals?*

Um, I'm adopted.
But we all live in Stony Stream... if that's what you mean?
Mea maxima.
click
My sincere apologies.
This must have been very troubling for you to witness.
I promise you won't remember a thing.
YO!
Put it down, mister.

What the hell, Kaje? We said we weren't going to bring that thing!
No, *you guys* said it...and I'm a crappy listener.
Let's all calm down, girls.
I give you my word that none of you will be harmed, and that the wounds of your injured companion will be addressed.
What does that *mean?*
Can these people fix Erin?
Children, your questions will be answered, but it's very dangerous for you to be out during Ablution.
If you would please just remain perfectly still, I can take you to--
BANG

BANG
BANG
BANG
NO!
Why... why did you...?
I didn't!
I didn't do anything!

Get back!
What is wrong with you alien dicks?!
This guy was going to help us!
Trust us, help is the last thing these old-timers would have given you.
And we're not aliens.
Then... what are you?
We're just like you.

We're teenagers.

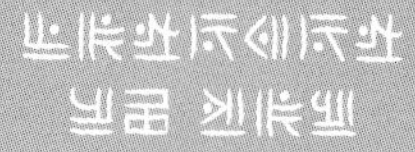

BRRIIING
BRRRRI--
Hello?
PUBLIC ENEMY

Aye up, *Cardinal* here.
Maxima for callz, sir, but troubles.
Alister's ben unmoored.
& de masters what did him hav ghosted.
Badder, they maytooken *stragglers.*
Bloody hell.
Best call down an Editrix.

An *Editrix?*
Grand Father, R ye poz?
Quite.
Can't risk another C-Day.
PUBLIC ENEMY
Stood.
Tasking 1 to de rhymescene now.
R killers canst *run*...
...but they willn't get far.

What's the holdup, ladies?
Let's keep moving.
Unless you want to take your chances out there with the old-timers?

We're not wading through another inch of this diarrhea until you tell us who you are and, and...and where you're taking Erin.
KJ, right? KJ, people call me Heck and my mate is Naldo.
And the sooner you quit waving that thing at us, the sooner we'll be able to get your friend to a device that can heal her.
That's what the last guy promised us...before you murdered him.
I didn't murder anyone.
I executed an evil son of a bitch.
Murder is what he did to my boyfriend.
Your...?
Eww.
Mac!
Don't worry about it.
You guys are from an effed-up time.

So Erin was right?
You're really, like...time travelers?
Well, *"travelers"* makes us sound like tourists... but close enough.
Hold on, if this is all for real, why don't you just turn back the clock to save your...whatever he was?
That's not how it works, Mac.
Your ending is your ending, no matter what.
But can we maybe start at the *beginning?*
When are you even from?
Thirteen.
Thirteen... the year?
Oh, right, we kinda rolled back the odometer after **Calamity** *ended all the--*
...papers...
...please don't forget... my papers...

Stay calm, new kid. We brought your bag, just like you begged.
Not that anybody's gonna care. Today's news pretty much blows this edition out of the--
AAAAOAAAAAOAOAO
No way, we're dirty. And these chicks somehow escaped the wash, too.
How could it even find us?
Slow down, how could what find us?
It's called an Editrix.
This won't translate, but it's a Poincaré construct that can...
...no.
Their stupid translator. It's been tracking us!
Heck, wait!
What are you so afraid of?!

P

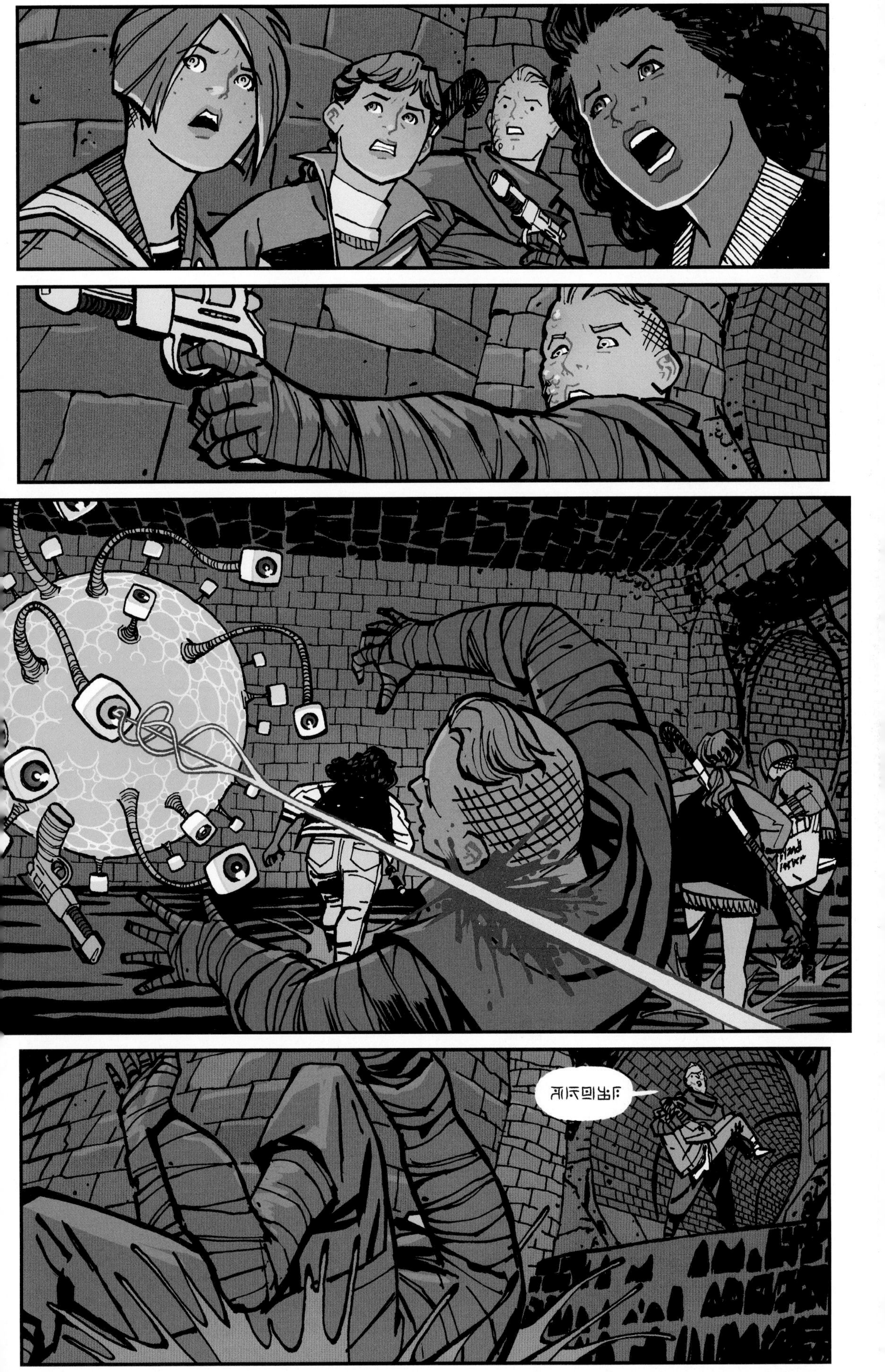

Shoot it!
I can't!
You definitely can!
I didn't bring any bullets!
I, I, I just wanted to make sure nobody else got--
HELP!
TIFF!
hng

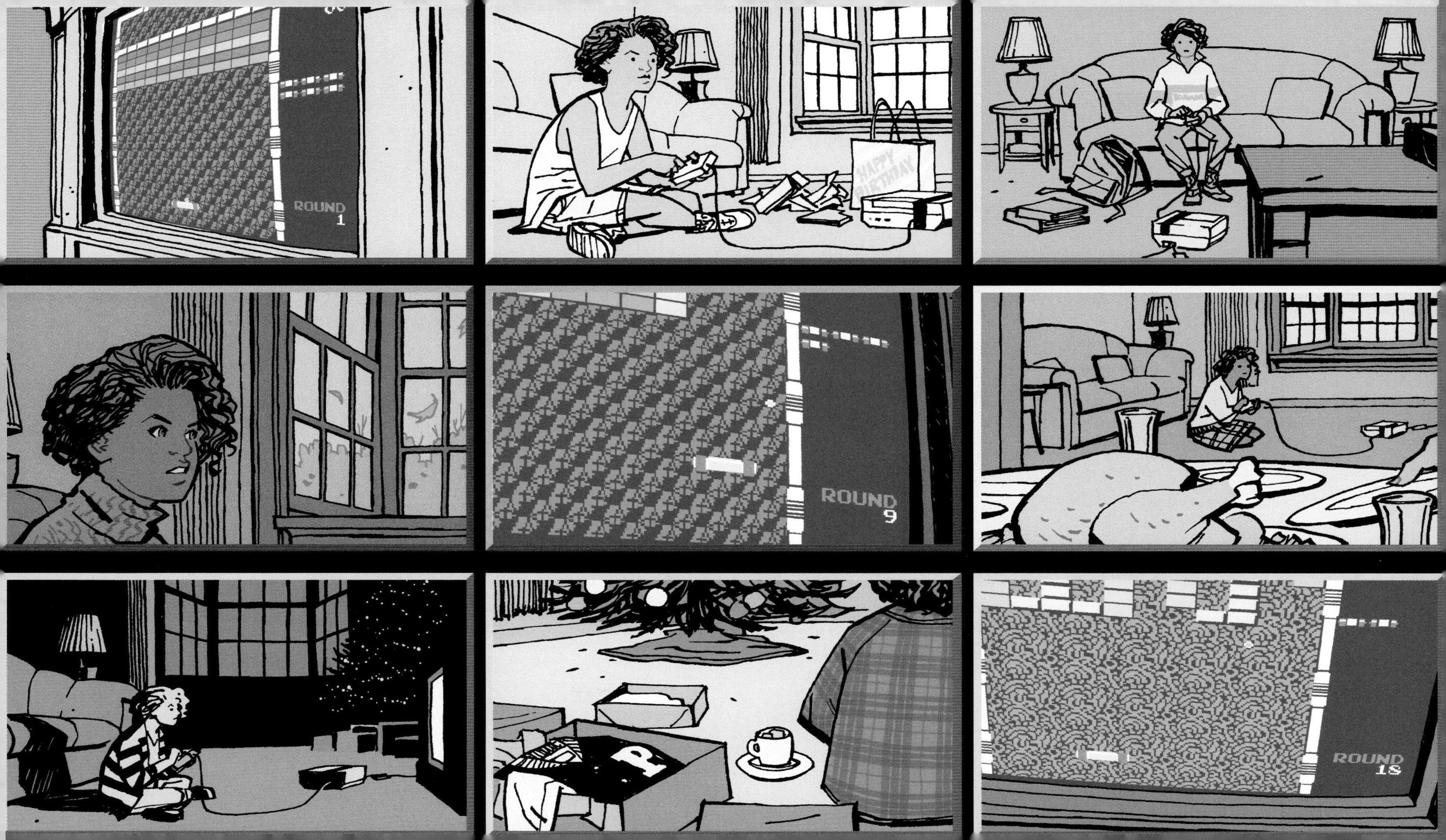
ROUND 1
HAPPY BIRTHDAY
ROUND 9
ROUND 18

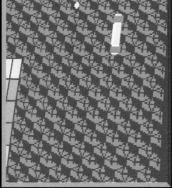

ROUND
21
ROUND
24

50190
PAUSE
ROUND
29
ROUND
35

ROUND
1
ROUND
30
HIGH
SCO
1030
795

uhk
LET GO!
KJ, don't!
AAAAOOOOOOOOO
AAAAAAAAAAAAAAA

I'm sorry
I'm sorry
I'm sorry
I'm sorry
I'm--
BANG
BANG
BANG
BANG
klick
klick
klick
klick

You're not dead?
Everybody's not dead...?
I'm guessing he just told us to *move.*
Kaje.
My... my *life* just flashed before my eyes.
No shit, but we're okay now, and we have to keep--
I mean, when that thing touched me, I started, like, *reliving* my past.
It was *hell.*
Most of it was just me playing the same dumb game. I didn't even think I liked it that much, but now I realize I...I basically *wasted* my entire existence.
God, I can still hear it.
I can still hear that crappy music.

Is that really such a good idea right now?
I'm sorry, did you not experience what we just experienced?
...why didn't I stop when I was stuck at Level 28...?
Fair.

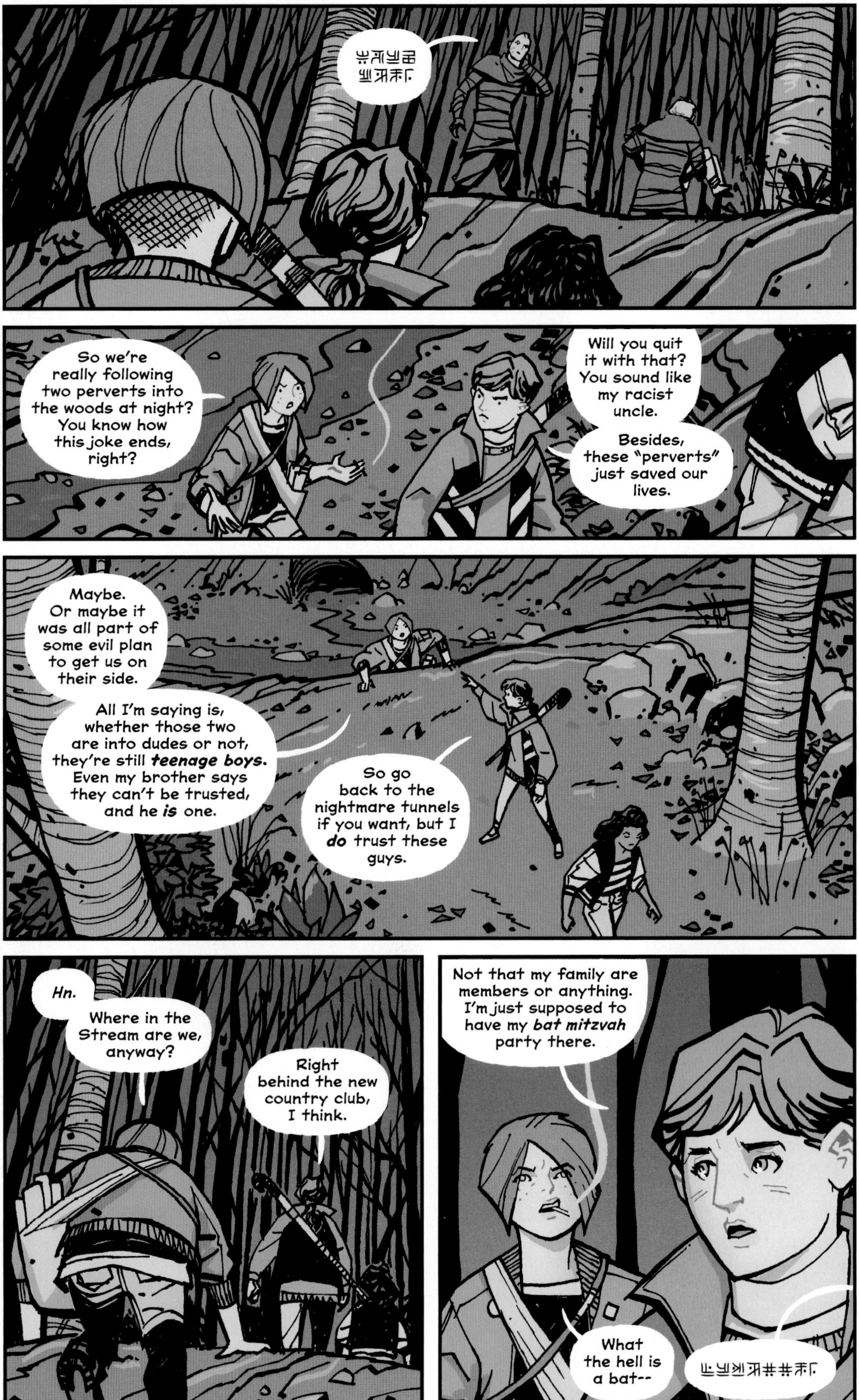

So we're really following two perverts into the woods at night? You know how this joke ends, right?
Will you quit it with that? You sound like my racist uncle.
Besides, these "perverts" just saved our lives.
Maybe. Or maybe it was all part of some evil plan to get us on their side.
All I'm saying is, whether those two are into dudes or not, they're still ***teenage boys.*** Even my brother says they can't be trusted, and he ***is*** one.
So go back to the nightmare tunnels if you want, but I ***do*** trust these guys.
Hn.
Where in the Stream are we, anyway?
Right behind the new country club, I think.
Not that my family are members or anything. I'm just supposed to have my ***bat mitzvah*** party there.
What the hell is a bat--

Is that...?
Looks exactly like the thing we found in that basement.
Your "device" can really make Erin better?

VSSSSSSSSS
This is mentally deranged.
They've probably got some kind of... futuristic first aid in there.
Like one of those MRI things, right?
...have to get...sixth bucket...
...for the... grand prize...
Wait, **he's** piling in, too?
Am I even awake right now?

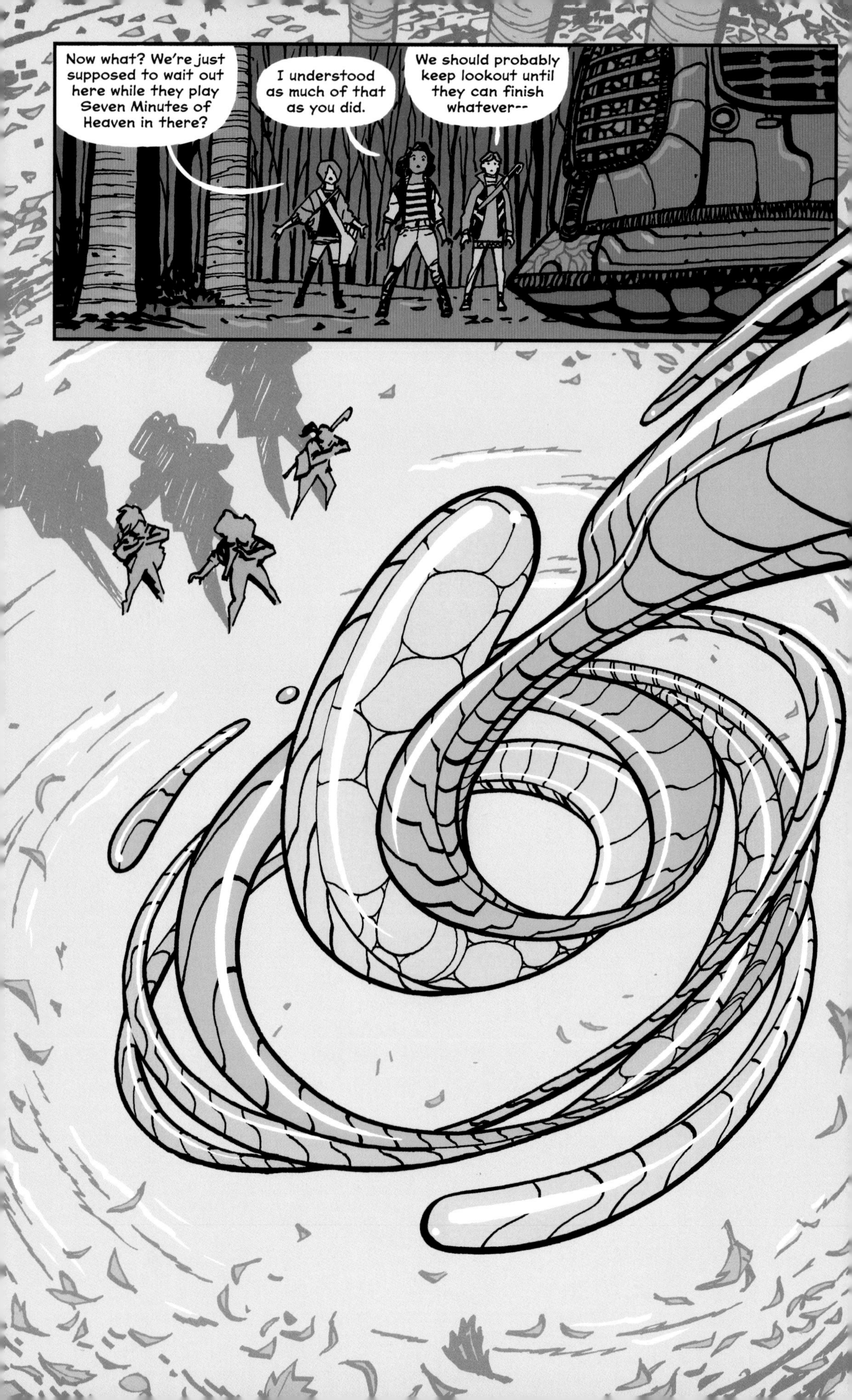
Now what? We're just supposed to wait out here while they play Seven Minutes of Heaven in there?
I understood as much of that as you did.
We should probably keep lookout until they can finish whatever--

Did.
Did they...?
Those lying assholes bailed on us!
They kidnapped Erin!
Oh, fuck.
I fucked up.

And now we're all alone.

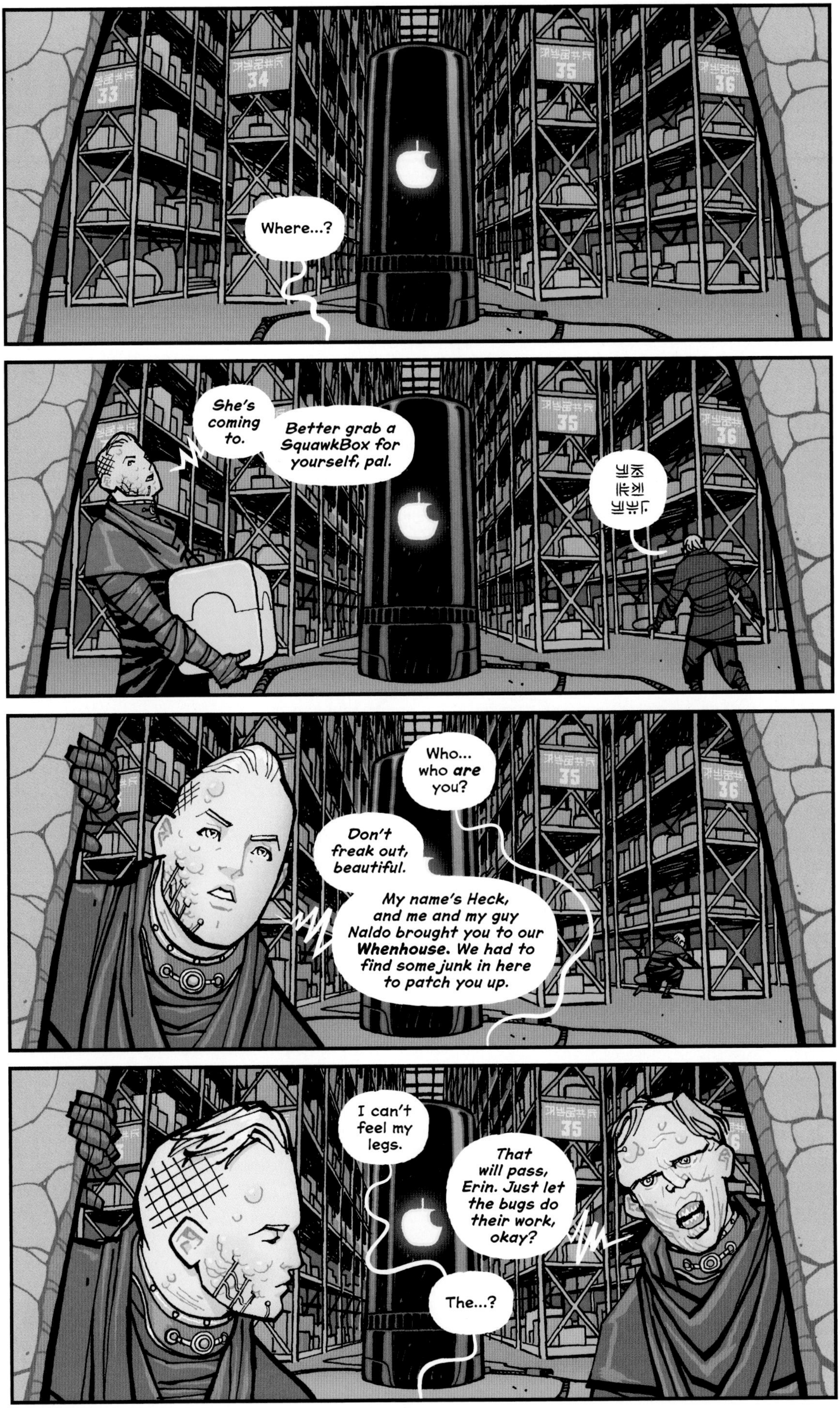
Where...?
She's coming to.
Better grab a SquawkBox for yourself, pal.
Who... who are you?
Don't freak out, beautiful.
My name's Heck, and me and my guy Naldo brought you to our Whenhouse. We had to find some junk in here to patch you up.
I can't feel my legs.
That will pass, Erin. Just let the bugs do their work, okay?
The...?

Oh.

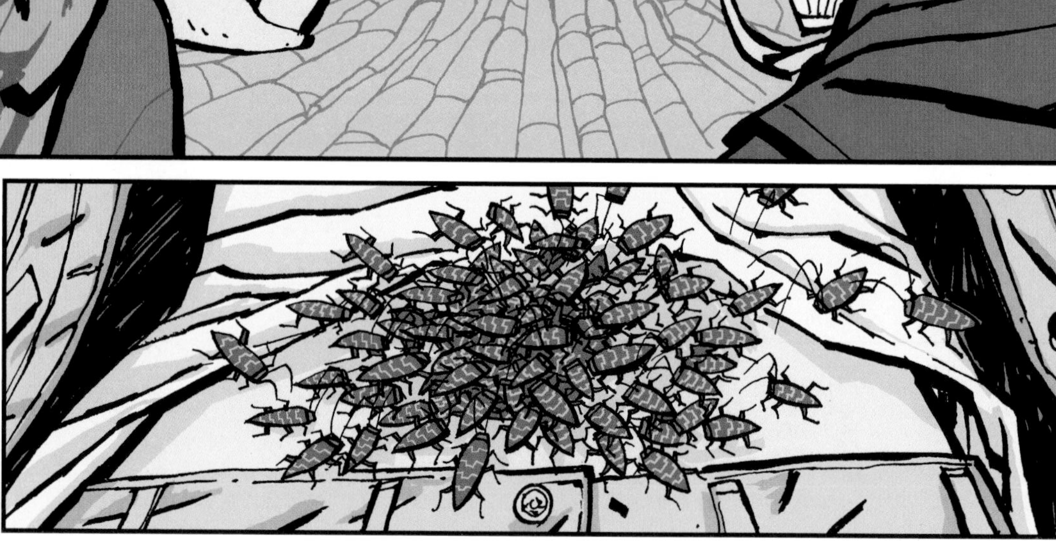

...I think I'm gonna throw up.
Not on the iNsecs!
You have no idea how hard those were to boost!
Right.
You're the guys who **stole** our walkie-talkie.
We're more **scavengers** than thieves, really.
"Yesterday's trash is tomorrow's treasure!"
Yeah, can you believe we found this badass spaceship in some dump?
Spaceship? I...I thought you were **time travelers.**
Well, since Earth never stops moving, it's a bad idea to travel through time without also considering **location.**
Say you're standing in the middle of Stony Stream and you jump straight back one hour, you'll just end up floating in the frozen vacuum where the planet is **about** to be.
Anyway, congrats, you're about to become an **astronaut.**
Cleveland Preserver

Sorry, I'm completely lost. Where *are* we?
About to rematerialize just above your mesosphere in '88.
Wait, is...is that today's Preserver?
COMICS
beep
OOF!
Tools of the trade. Long story.
All that matters is that we're getting you back to your **friends.**
They're not my friends, they're just... just the people who **shot** me.
Oh, no.
It's the old-timers.
They're trying to ground us!
Holy shit.
We're gonna have to **break curfew.**

Messing with the tributary like that is suicide!
So is staying put and letting those assholes blast apart our chute.
Hang on, I'm gonna try to shift us somewhere beneath them...
Please, Holy Mary, I just want to make it to college and have my own--

Wait a goddamn second.
The ***basement.***
...is this a game, too? Am I in it all over again...?
Mac, listen, we have to get back to where we first saw one of those... whatever the hell it was that just disappeared.
Why? You think we can use that ***other*** capsule-thing to chase after the one they used to kidnap Erin?
No, I'm thinking there never ***was*** an other.
What if the capsule-thing we found this morning was the exact ***same*** capsule-thing those guys just left in with the new kid?
I actually get what Kaje is saying.
If those guys really came here from the ***future,*** maybe that weird escape pod of theirs could--
Aweful deep waterz, lassie.

Come ashore peacenik now, aye?
JESUS CHRIST!
Please don't kill us!
We... we totally give up!
Actually.
We don't.

Tiffany, what are you--
I'm not going to stand here and be eaten by some bitch's **dinosaur.** I am finally **doing** something with my life.
No more *Arkanoid,* got it?
Arkawho?
Stay back!
Common, grrl, clear yain't de kind what can **end** a human's being.
If you're saying I can't kill a person, you're...you're probably right.
But I've got no problem killing **it.**
AWWWRK

Drop the magic wand or I swear to God on the Holy Bible I will shoot your pet in the *neck.*
Lies.
Ye... ye wood never.
kachick
Aight!
Begging.
Just... just unharm my girl.
Ha, *smooth move,* Ex-Lax.
That gun isn't even *loaded.*
Dummy, why would you--
BADEET!

KRAKOOM
RAAK
What... what just...?
I don't know, but you should *not* be allowed to touch stuff that can accidentally shoot people.
You think she's all right?
I think we should get the hell out of here.
Before her *friends* show up.
...hnn...

Mea culpa, Grand Father.
Mea *maxima* culpa, but... but--
Stop apologizing and tell me plainly, Cardinal.
Apple Records
De yung locals b harmed & dangereux.
Nochoiced but to try as *adults.*
Permission de charge ultimo?
Denied.
I'll punish them myself.

Daddy?
Are you *crying?*
John Lennon
1940-1980
Yes, Erin.
Why are you sad?
I'm more *afraid* than sad.
I...I didn't know grownups got scared, too.
Oh, honey.
We're terrified.

hhhh
I'm alive.
I'm really--
...hey...
...you're awake...

no
...ship kept us... all in stasis... long as it could...
...but I'm worried... our storage cells... coulda cracked... so you need to... vamoose...
I don't even know you people.
Why did you do all this for me?
...you girls... reminded us... of us...
...kids just trying.... to make a living... are always...the good guys...
I don't know what to do.
...go help... your crew...
...like my moms... used to say... a working man... always does right... by his...

Heck...?
How do
I get out of
this thing?!
AHHH!
Erin?

Holy crap, I was right!
Back up, does that mean new girl was in there the whole time she was also down here with--
Who cares, she's *here.*
Those fruitcakes didn't hurt you, did they?
...no.
Heck and Naldo *saved* me.
And now they're dead.

What?
Those guys died... fixing *my* mistake?
Erin, I'm so--
Whatever is going on here is none of our fault, all right?
And it was... it was cool of you guys to come find me, but that thing had some kind of ***fuel leak,*** so we can't stay down here.
I don't know how much you remember, but things aren't exactly much safer out there.
Girls!
I know you're in there!
Who the eff is ***that?***

Listen to your elders and come outside this instant!
Apple Records
I'm sure you're confused, but whatever those ***juvenile delinquents*** in there told you is completely untrue.
You have waded deep into a very old... generational conflict.
Those boys fancy themselves Robin Hoods, stealing from the past to fund the future, but they're just a murderous gang of thugs.
Get far away from them before someone gets ***hurt.***

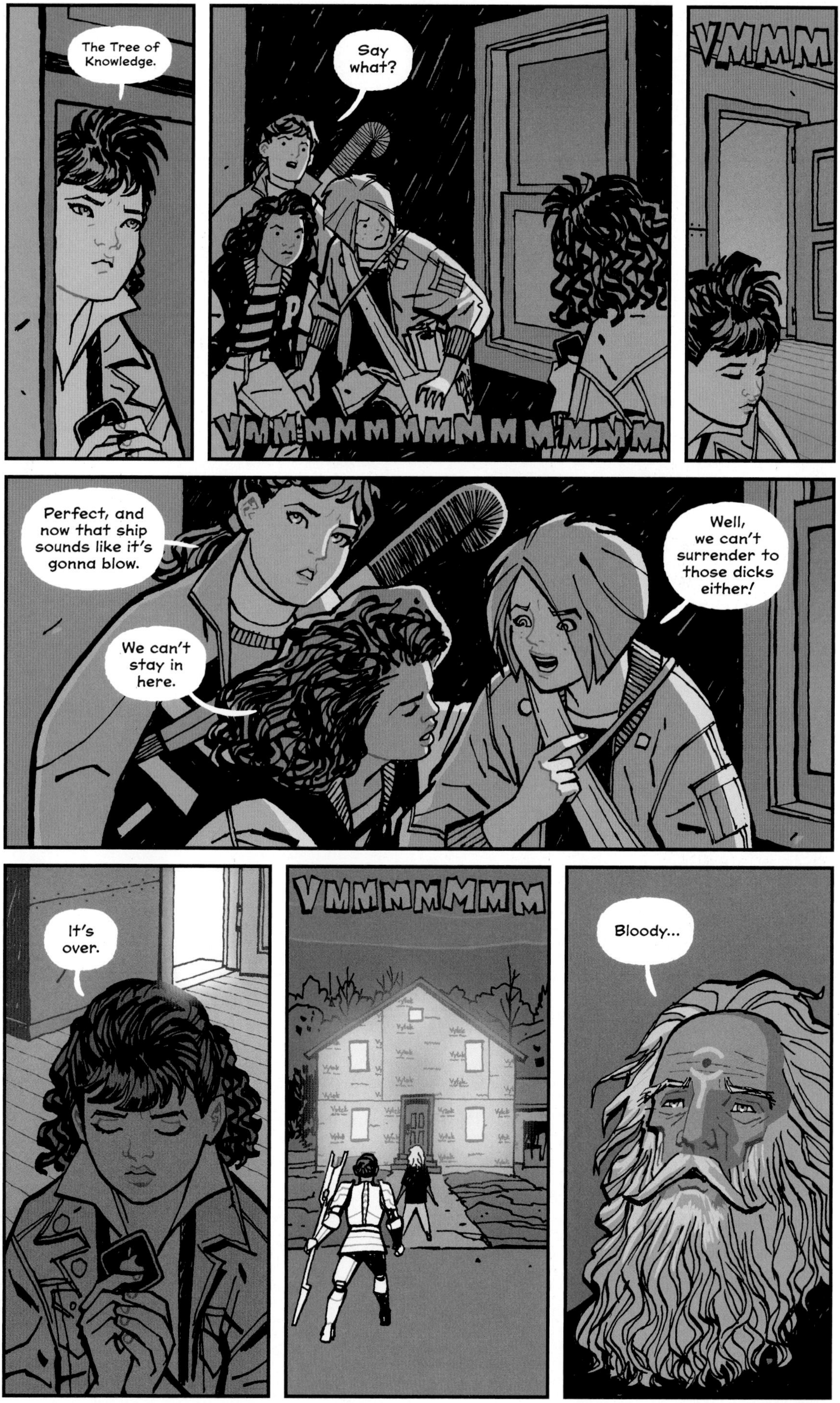
The Tree of Knowledge.
Say what?
VMMMMMMMMMMMMMMMM
VMMM
Perfect, and now that ship sounds like it's gonna blow.
We can't stay in here.
Well, we can't surrender to those dicks either!
It's over.
VMMMMMMM
Bloody...

HUHN
Mac!
What... what just happened?
Where'd everything go?
More importantly, where's KJ?

um
Car.
And I lost our stupid gun.
It's slowing down. What do we do?
What the Preserver taught us.
Excuse me!
My name is Erin Tieng, I deliver newspapers, and...and my friends and I need help, please.
Is this a joke?

My name is Erin Tieng.
TO BE CONTINUED